Daniel Dinosaur

Written by
Daryl K. Cobb

Illustrated by
Carla F. Castagno

To: Tristan!
Have Fun reading.
Daryl K Cobb

*I give thanks everyday
for the two little people
who inspire me.*

Daryl K. Cobb

*I dedicate all my pictures
to my son, Andrea,
and especially
to my husband, Roberto.*

Carla F. Castagno

Daniel, Daniel Dinosaur
stood sixty feet
and maybe more.
He dined on trees
of leafy greens.

He bathed in streams
till squeaky clean.

Daniel, he had just turned four -

he played

and played

and played some more.

One of his favorite things to do
was play hide and seek
with his sister Sue.

One day he was left in charge
while his mommy was away.
Suzy said to Daniel,
"Let's go to the stream and play."

His mom and dad had told him,
"No matter what you do,
you can play till we get home,
don't take your eyes off Sue."

Daniel, he got hungry,
for a second he turned away.

He grabbed a snack,
and when he turned back
Suzy had walked away.

Daniel then looked high and low,
looked everywhere
he thought she'd go.

He looked down the stream
and in between.

Now what was he to do?
He could not find
his sister Sue.

Daniel then began to cry.

He knew that time
was passing by.

"Daniel, Daniel Dinosaur!"
a voice said from behind.

"I am too good at this game,
you seek but you cannot find."

Daniel quickly turned around
and there stood Sister Sue.

She was playing hide and seek.
She thought he was too.

Now no matter
where they go
or whatever
they may do,
Daniel never
takes his eyes off
his little sister Sue.